This book
belongs to

....

LADYBIRD  TALES

CLASSIC STORIES TO SHARE

LADYBIRD BOOKS

UK | USA | Canada | Ireland | Australia
India | New Zealand | South Africa

Ladybird Books is part of the Penguin Random House group of companies
whose addresses can be found at global.penguinrandomhouse.com.

ladybird.com

First published 2015
001

Copyright © Ladybird Books Ltd, 2015
Cover illustration by Gail Yerrill

Titles previously available as:
Ladybird Tales: Hansel and Gretel copyright © Ladybird Books Ltd 2012
Ladybird Tales: Aladdin copyright © Ladybird Books 2014
Ladybird Tales: Cinderella copyright © Ladybird Books Ltd 2012
Ladybird Tales: Snow White and the Seven Dwarfs copyright © Ladybird Books Ltd 2012
Ladybird Tales: Puss in Boots copyright © Ladybird Books Ltd 2012

Printed in China

A CIP catalogue record for this book is available from the British Library

ISBN: 978–0–723–29906–6

LADYBIRD TALES

CLASSIC STORIES TO SHARE

Contents

Hansel and Gretel

A story showing the unbreakable bond between a brother and his sister. When Hansel and Gretel meet a witch, only their quick wits can save them.

Aladdin

A tale of a poor boy who is tricked by a greedy magician in search of a magic lamp.

Cinderella

A tale about a beautiful girl who enchants a handsome prince. When Cinderella's fairy godmother waves her magic wand, anything can happen.

Page 97

Puss in Boots

A story of a clever cat who, with his boots and his bag, helps his master overcome his troubles after his father dies.

Page 139

Snow White
and the Seven Dwarfs

A magical story about a beautiful princess and the dwarfs who save her from a jealous queen.

Page 181

Hansel
and Gretel

Retold by Vera Southgate M.A., B.COM
with illustrations by Adrienne Salgado

ONCE UPON A TIME there were two children, a boy called Hansel and a girl called Gretel. They lived with their father and stepmother in a little cottage at the edge of a forest.

Their father was a woodcutter, and he was very poor. One day, he had so little money that he could no longer give his family enough to eat. This made him very unhappy.

"How can we feed the children?" he asked his wife one night. "We have just enough for two, but not for four."

15

His wife did not really like the children.
"I know what we must do," she replied.
"Tomorrow we will take the children into
the thickest part of the forest. Then we must
leave them there. They will never find their
way home. We shall be free of them!"

"I could never do that," said the woodcutter.
"How can you even think of such a thing?"

"You fool!" his wife cried. "Then all four
of us will die of hunger!"

The woodcutter's wife gave him no peace,
until at last he agreed.

Too hungry to sleep, Hansel and Gretel overheard what was said. Gretel cried bitterly.

"Don't worry," said Hansel. "I will look after you."

Once his parents were asleep, he crept quietly outside. White pebbles lay around, like silver coins in the moonlight. He filled his pockets with them, and went back to bed.

Early next morning, the woodcutter's wife wakened the two children. "We are going into the forest to chop wood," she told them.

As they walked along, Hansel kept glancing back at the cottage. "Hansel, why are you lagging behind?" asked his father.

"My white cat is on the roof, Father," said Hansel. "I am trying to say goodbye."

"It's the sun shining on the white chimney, you silly boy," said his stepmother.

But Hansel wasn't really looking at a cat. Each time he stopped, he dropped a pebble from his pocket onto the path.

When they came to the middle of the forest, the woodcutter said, "I will make a fire so you won't be cold."

"We are going to chop wood," their stepmother said. "We will come for you when we are ready."

Hansel and Gretel sat by the fire.
Then they waited for their parents to come.
They waited so long that they fell asleep.

When they woke, it was dark. Gretel was frightened.

"Wait until the moon comes up," Hansel comforted her. "Then we will find our way home."

At last the moon rose in the sky. Hansel took his sister's hand, and followed the pebbles he had left on the path. They shone like silver coins in the moonlight and showed the children the way home.

"You naughty children!" scolded their stepmother. "Where have you been?"

The woodcutter was very happy to see them. It had broken his heart to leave them in the forest.

Before long, the family had very little food again. One night the children heard their stepmother talking to their father.

"We have half a loaf of bread left," she told him. "Once that is gone, we will have nothing. We must take the children deeper into the forest. This time they must not find their way home!"

The woodcutter's heart was heavy. He would rather have shared his last crust with his children. But his wife would not listen to his pleading, and again he had to agree.

As soon as the woodcutter and his wife were asleep, Hansel got up to fill his pockets with pebbles as before. But his stepmother had locked the door. Sadly, he went back to bed.

"Don't cry, Gretel," he said bravely. "All will be well, you'll see."

Early next morning, the stepmother wakened the children. Before they left for the forest, she gave them each a very small piece of bread.

As they walked through the trees, Hansel lagged behind and stopped every now and then.

"Hansel, why do you keep stopping?" his father asked.

"I'm looking back at my little dove," Hansel replied. "He's nodding goodbye to me."

"That isn't a dove, you foolish boy," said the stepmother. "It's the sun, shining on the chimney." But Hansel wasn't looking at the dove. Each time he stopped, he dropped a crumb of bread on to the path.

The woodcutter's wife led the children to a part of the forest they didn't know. "Stay here," she told them. "We're going into the forest to cut wood. We'll fetch you in the evening."

At noon, Gretel shared her small piece of bread with Hansel and they lay down to wait. But when evening arrived no one came.

"Don't be afraid, Gretel," Hansel said. "When the moon comes up, we will see the crumbs of bread I dropped. They will lead us home."

Soon the moon shone, but they couldn't see any crumbs. The birds had eaten them all!

Hansel and Gretel walked all night, and all the next day, and they were still deep in the forest. They were so tired they could go no further, and they lay down under a tree to sleep.

Next morning, the children walked on. They were very hungry. By midday Hansel felt they must get help soon, or they would die of hunger.

Just then a beautiful white bird perched on a nearby branch. It sang so sweetly that they followed it as it flew through the trees. The bird led them straight to a little cottage!

"Look, Hansel!" cried Gretel. "The cottage is made of bread and cakes, and the windows are made of sugar!"

Hansel broke off a piece of bread. Gretel took a bite from one of the cakes. Soon they were both munching happily.

Just then, the door opened and out came an old woman, walking on crutches.

Hansel and Gretel were so frightened, they dropped what they were eating. But the old woman smiled at them. "Come in, children!" she said.

She led them inside the little cottage. A meal of pancakes, milk and fruit lay ready on the table. In the back room were two little beds. After they had eaten, the children lay down, happy to be safe at last.

Hansel and Gretel did not know that the old woman was really a wicked old witch, who trapped children. She couldn't see very well, but she had a fine sense of smell. She could smell children coming.

The house of bread and cakes had been built to tempt children in.

The witch gave an evil laugh. "These two shall not escape!" she cackled.

Early next morning, the witch pulled Hansel from his bed, and locked him in a cage. Although he screamed, there was no one to help him.

Gretel came next. "Get up, you lazy girl!" screeched the witch. "Cook something good for your brother. He will stay in the cage until he is fat enough for me to eat!"

Gretel began to cry, but the wicked witch only laughed at her tears.

Day after day passed. Gretel was soon tired out, for the witch made her clean and scrub, and cook huge meals for poor Hansel.

Every morning the witch went up to the cage. "Hold out your finger, Hansel," she would cackle. "Let me feel if you are fat enough to eat."

But Hansel would hold out a bone instead. The witch had such bad eyesight that she always thought it was his finger. She wondered why it grew no fatter.

Four weeks passed. Because of Hansel's clever trick, the witch thought he was still very thin. Soon she lost her patience.

"Fetch some water, Gretel!" she shrieked angrily. "This morning I will kill Hansel, and cook him." The tears ran down Gretel's face.

"First of all, we'll bake some bread," the old witch said with a sly look at Gretel. "I have already made the dough and heated the oven."

She pushed Gretel up to the oven door. "Go on," said the witch. "See if it's hot enough. Then we'll put the bread in."

But she really planned to put Gretel in the oven to bake. Then she would eat the little girl as well as Hansel.

Gretel had guessed what the wicked witch was thinking. "I can't go in there," she said. "I'm too big."

"You silly child," the witch said angrily. "Look, I could even get in myself!"

She bent down and put her head into the oven. Gretel gave her a hard push, and she fell right inside.

Shutting the iron door, Gretel bolted it. The witch couldn't get out.

Gretel ran to Hansel's cage. "The witch is dead!" she cried. "We're safe! Now I must get you out of that cage."

Gretel couldn't find the key, so she broke the lock with a poker from the fireplace. The door swung open. Hansel sprang out, like a bird from a cage. They hugged one another over and over again.

Now they had nothing to fear. And when they looked over the witch's house, they found caskets of pearls and precious stones.

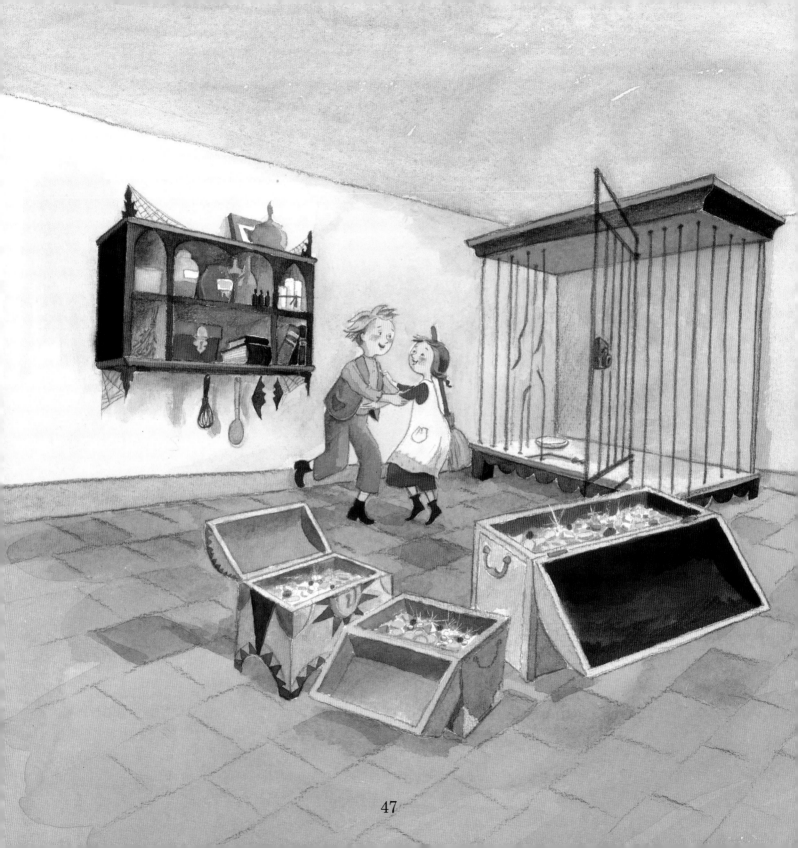

"These are better than pebbles!" said Hansel. He put as many into his pockets as they would hold. Gretel filled her apron.

They left the witch's cottage and walked away through the trees. It was dark in the forest, but when they were lost the friendly birds and animals showed them the way.

At last, Hansel and Gretel came to a part of the forest they knew.

They began to run, and at last came to their own home. Inside, they ran into their father's arms.

He had not had one happy moment since the children had been left in the forest. He was alone now, for their stepmother had died. "I'm so glad you've come home," he said.

Gretel shook out her apron, and pearls and diamonds rolled all over the floor. Hansel threw out one handful after another from his pockets.

Their troubles were over. From then on, the woodcutter and his children all lived happily ever after.

Aladdin

Retold by Marie Stuart
with illustrations by Kou Lan

LONG AGO, in China, there lived a poor tailor named Mustafa who had a son called Aladdin.

When Mustafa fell ill and died, Aladdin's mother had to do all the work instead. Aladdin would never help.

One day, when Aladdin was out playing, a man asked him if he knew Mustafa the tailor.

"He was my father," said Aladdin, "but he is dead. Why do you ask?"

"He was my brother," the man replied. "Now that I have found you I want to help you and your mother."

"Here is some money for your mother," said Aladdin's uncle. "Tell her I will see her soon."

The next day, Aladdin saw the man again, and he invited himself to Aladdin's house for dinner.

"Here is some more money for your mother to buy something nice for us to eat," he said.

Aladdin took the money home to her.

When the man came to their house, Aladdin's mother said, "My husband never said he had a brother."

The man was not really Aladdin's uncle but a magician.

"What work do you do?" the magician asked Aladdin.

"He just plays with the other boys all day," replied Aladdin's mother.

"Then I shall buy you a shop to look after," declared the man.

Next morning, the magician took Aladdin shopping. He bought him some new clothes. The following day, they went to look at big houses with lovely gardens. Aladdin liked them very much.

"One day I shall buy one," promised the magician. "But let us sit and have something to eat. We have walked a long way."

The magician fed Aladdin all the cakes and sweets he could eat. Then he said, "Let's look at the best garden of all before we go back."

When they had gone a little way, he cried, "Stop! This is the place."

The magician lit a fire with dry sticks, and put something on it that made black smoke. Then, all at once, Aladdin saw a big stone with a ring in it under his feet.

"Pull it," said the magician.

Aladdin pulled, and up came the stone. Then he saw that it had been on top of a well. It was very black inside the well and he did not like the look of it.

The magician pointed into the darkness. He said, "If you go down there and do everything I say, you will be rich."

Aladdin nodded eagerly.

"You will find a door," explained the magician. "Open it and go through. You will come to a large cave and some boxes of money. Do not take them."

"Why not?" asked Aladdin.

"Do as I say!" the magician answered angrily. Then he said, "Go on until you come to another cave, and then another. You will see boxes of gold and silver in these, but do not take any."

"When you leave the last cave, you will see
a fine garden. At the end of it will be a table
with a lamp on it. Bring me the lamp. You can
have anything you wish from the garden,"
said the magician.

Then he took off a ring and gave it to Aladdin.

"This may be of use if you need help," he
added. "Now go!"

Aladdin went down into the dark well. Down,
down he went!

Everything was just as the magician had said.
He touched nothing in any of the caves, and
went through a door into the garden.

There, Aladdin found the lamp. He took it and then looked around. Every tree was encrusted with rich jewels – red, blue, green, gold and white.

Aladdin put down the lamp and took all the jewels he could. Even when he could carry no more, there were still many left on the trees.

"I shall come back again one day," he thought, "but now I must take this lamp to my uncle."

So Aladdin left the garden and went back the way he had come.

When he got to the top of the well he could see the magician.

"Help me out, please!" Aladdin called up to him.

"Give me the lamp first," said the magician, "then you can use both hands."

But Aladdin answered, "No! Not until I get out."

The magician was very angry. He put something on the fire again and said some magic words. At once, the stone moved back into place over the well, trapping Aladdin inside.

"Wait!" he called. "I will give you the lamp if only you will help me out!"

But the magician had gone.

It was no use calling, so Aladdin tried to go back into the garden. But the door was shut tight. He sat down in the darkness and cried. For three days he had nothing to eat or drink.

"I wish I had a little fire to warm me!" he said.

He rubbed his hands and, as he did so, he rubbed the ring that the magician had given him.

"I am the slave of the ring," said a voice. "I will come whenever you rub the ring and will do anything you ask. What do you want?"

"Please take me home," begged Aladdin.

No sooner had he said this than he found that he was home!

His mother cried, "Here you are at last! I thought you were lost!"

She gave him something to eat and drink, and he went to bed. The next day she said, "There is nothing left for us to eat."

But Aladdin said, "I am hungry. I shall go and see if someone will buy some of these jewels or this lamp from me."

"It looks so old," replied his mother. "Let me give it a rub first. I shall soon make it look like new. Then you will get more money for it."

Aladdin's mother took the lamp and gave it a rub. Suddenly, there was a puff of smoke, and a strange-looking man appeared. He bowed and said, "I am the slave of the lamp."

Aladdin's mother dropped the lamp in fright.

"Don't be afraid!" cried Aladdin, picking up the lamp.

Then the strange man said, "The lamp you are holding is a magic one. Whenever you rub it, I will appear and do whatever you ask."

As they were both very hungry, Aladdin said, "Please bring us something to eat and drink."

The slave of the lamp clapped his hands and a fine dinner appeared on gold plates.

When everything had been eaten, Aladdin said to his mother, "I will go to the shop and sell these plates. The money I get for them will last us a long time."

But soon that money had been spent, so Aladdin rubbed the lamp again. At once, the slave appeared and gave him everything he and his mother needed.

This went on for three or four years. By that time Aladdin was no longer a boy. He had become a man, and a very handsome one!

One day in the street, Aladdin saw a princess on horseback and fell in love at once.

"I want to marry her," he told his mother.

"We must ask the king," she replied.

Aladdin's mother took him the last of the jewels Aladdin had found. "My son loves the princess," she said. "He sends you this gift."

"He must be a very important man!" cried the king, and he promised that Aladdin could marry the princess.

Aladdin's mother went home to tell Aladdin the good news.

But a rich man said to the king, "My son will give you much more if he can marry your daughter."

When Aladdin found this out, he rubbed the lamp.

The slave appeared and Aladdin said angrily, "Bring the princess and the rich man's son to me."

The slave did as Aladdin asked him. The man was shut in a dark room. Then Aladdin told the princess of his love for her, and how her father had promised that she could marry him.

Then the slave took her and the rich man's son back to the palace.

The rich man's son was so scared that he wouldn't marry the princess. The slave told Aladdin this. Aladdin said, "Bring me many bags of gold and jewels, and some slaves to carry them to the king."

Aladdin's mother went with the slaves, giving money to all the people on the way to the palace.

When the king looked inside the bags of gold and jewels, he cried, "Now I will let your son marry my daughter! Tell him to come here at once."

Before Aladdin went to see the king, he rubbed the lamp and said to the slave, "Bring me new clothes made of the richest cloth in the land, and a fine, white horse."

Aladdin looked just like a prince on a horse, and the princess fell in love at once.

"Before I marry her, I must have a house," said Aladdin.

That night, he rubbed the lamp and said to the slave, "Make me the best house that anyone has ever seen!"

The next morning, a beautiful house appeared, right next to the king's own palace. Aladdin married the princess, and they lived happily in their new home for a year or two. Then one day the magician came back.

When the magician found that Aladdin was alive and that he was now a prince, he was very cross.

"I must get the magic lamp away from him," he thought.

He bought some new lamps from a shop. Then he walked up and down the streets calling out, "New lamps for old! New lamps for old!"

One of the princess's women ran indoors to tell her mistress.

"Aladdin has an old lamp," thought the princess. "He will be pleased to get a new one for it."

The princess gave it to the magician in return for a new one. She planned to surprise Aladdin.

As soon as the magician had the lamp, he hid where no one could see him and gave it a rub.

The slave appeared and the magician said, "Take Aladdin's house away."

The next morning, Aladdin's house was gone.

The king sent his men to find Aladdin. They pulled him from his horse and took him to the king.

"Where is the princess?" cried the king.

"She is at home," Aladdin replied.

"But your home is gone," said the king. "Bring the princess back or you must die."

Aladdin could not get his lamp because his house had gone, so he rubbed his magic ring.

"Take me to the princess," said Aladdin to the slave of the ring.

Suddenly, he was in his house with the princess. She told him about the old man with the lamps.

"That man is a wicked magician," said Aladdin. "I must get the lamp back from him quickly!"

He gave the princess a little bag and said to her, "Ask the magician to supper. When he is not looking, empty this into his cup."

The princess did as she was told, and the magician fell back dead.

Aladdin picked up the lamp and rubbed it. When the slave appeared, Aladdin ordered, "Take us and our home back to where it was before."

The king looked out of the palace window. "The princess and Aladdin are back!" he said to the queen. They rushed to see the princess.

"I am so glad to be back," she cried. "A wicked magician took me away, but he is dead now. Dear Aladdin found me. I love him very much and you must love him, too."

The king and queen agreed to do so, and they all lived happily ever after.

95

Cinderella

Retold by Vera Southgate M.A., B.COM
with illustrations by Yunhee Park

ONCE UPON A TIME there was a little girl called Cinderella. Her mother was dead and she lived with her father and two stepsisters.

Cinderella's stepsisters were fair of face but, because they were bad-tempered and unkind, their faces grew to look ugly.

They were jealous of Cinderella because she was a lovely child, and so they were often unkind to her.

The stepsisters made Cinderella do all the work in the house. She worked from morning till night without stopping.

99

Cinderella not only did all the housework, but she also helped her stepsisters to dress. She cleaned their shoes, brushed their hair, tied their ribbons and fastened their buckles.

The sisters had many fine clothes, but all Cinderella had was an old dress and a pair of wooden shoes.

After she had worked until she was weary, Cinderella had no bed to go to. She had to sleep by the hearth in the cinders. That was why her stepsisters called her Cinderella and that was why she always looked dusty and dirty.

Now it happened that the king arranged a great feast for his son. The feast was to last three days and on each evening there was to be a grand ball. All the beautiful young girls in the country were invited, in order that the prince might choose himself a bride.

Cinderella's stepsisters were invited to the feast. Cinderella was not invited. Everyone thought that she was her sisters' maid.

On the evening of the first ball, Cinderella had to help her sisters to get dressed. Cinderella thought of how she would like to go to the ball and tears began to run down her face.

"I would like to wear a beautiful dress and go to the ball," said Cinderella.

"A fine sight you would be at a ball!" laughed the stepsisters.

When they had left, poor Cinderella sat down and cried. Suddenly, she heard a voice saying, "What is the matter, my dear?" There stood her fairy godmother, smiling kindly at her.

"I would like to go to the ball," said Cinderella.

"And so you shall, my dear," said her fairy godmother. "Dry your eyes and then do exactly as I tell you."

"First, go into the garden and bring me the biggest pumpkin you can find," said the fairy godmother.

"Very well," said Cinderella and she ran off to the garden. She picked the biggest pumpkin she could find and took it to her fairy godmother.

The fairy godmother touched the pumpkin with her magic wand. Immediately, it turned into the most wonderful golden carriage you can imagine. The inside was lined with red velvet.

"Now run and fetch me the mousetrap from the pantry," said the fairy godmother.

Cinderella ran off to the pantry. She found the mousetrap on the floor. There were six mice in it.

Cinderella brought the mousetrap to her fairy godmother. One touch of the magic wand and the mice turned into six fine grey horses.

"Next, fetch me the rat trap from the cellar," said the fairy godmother.

Cinderella ran down the steps to the cellar. She found the rat trap, with one rat in it, and took it to her fairy godmother.

One touch of the fairy wand and the rat changed into a smart coachman, dressed in red livery trimmed with gold braid.

"Lastly," said Cinderella's fairy godmother, "I want you to bring me the two lizards that are behind the cucumber frame at the bottom of the garden."

Cinderella ran into the garden and there she found two small lizards.

Cinderella's fairy godmother touched the lizards with her fairy wand. They turned into two smart footmen.

There was now a golden coach, lined with red velvet, drawn by six grey horses. There was a coachman, in red livery, to drive the coach, and two fine footmen to open the doors.

Cinderella glanced down at her old, tattered dress and her wooden shoes.

"One more touch of my magic wand, my dear," said her fairy godmother. Then there happened the most wonderful magic of all.

Cinderella found herself in a beautiful ballgown of pale pink silk. On her feet were dainty pink slippers. Cinderella's face was shining with joy. "Oh! Thank you!" she cried.

"Enjoy yourself at the ball, my dear," said her fairy godmother. "But remember, you must be home before the clock strikes midnight. For, on the last stroke of twelve, all will be as it was before and yourself the ragged girl you were."

The footman opened the door of the carriage. Cinderella sat down on the red velvet cushions. Then they were off.

When Cinderella arrived at the palace, she looked so beautiful that her sisters did not know her.

The prince thought that he had never seen such a beautiful princess. He took her hand and danced with her all evening. He never let her out of his sight.

Cinderella had never spent such a wonderful evening in her whole life. Yet she still remembered her fairy godmother's warning.

At a quarter to twelve, Cinderella left the ballroom while the other guests were still dancing. Her carriage was waiting for her and she was driven quickly home. She arrived at the door just as the clock was striking twelve.

On the last stroke of midnight, the coach became a pumpkin, the horses became mice, the coachman a rat, and the footmen lizards. Cinderella's ballgown vanished and she found herself once more in her old grey dress and wooden shoes.

When her stepsisters returned home they could talk about nothing but the beautiful princess at the ball. Cinderella listened but said nothing.

On the second evening, the stepsisters went off to the ball, leaving Cinderella sitting by the fire.

No sooner had they gone than Cinderella's fairy godmother appeared again. Just as before, her magic wand produced the golden carriage with its coachman and footmen.

This time Cinderella's ballgown was even more beautiful than on the first evening. It was made of pale blue satin, with floating overskirts of pale blue net embroidered with silver thread. Her pale blue slippers were embroidered in silver.

Once more, Cinderella's fairy godmother reminded her to be home by midnight.

When Cinderella arrived at the ball in the blue dress, everyone was astonished at her beauty. The prince had waited for her and he instantly took her by the hand. As before, he danced with no one but her.

Cinderella was so happy that she almost forgot what her fairy godmother had told her. Suddenly, it was five minutes to twelve. She left the prince and hurried out of the ballroom as quickly as she could.

Cinderella's carriage was waiting. But they were only halfway home when the clock began to strike twelve.

On the last stroke of midnight, Cinderella found herself in her old grey dress and wooden shoes in the middle of a dark, lonely road.

She had to run the rest of the way home as fast as she could. Even so, she had just seated herself on her stool by the cinders when her sisters returned from the ball.

Once more, all the stepsisters could talk about was the beautiful stranger with whom the prince had danced.

On the evening of the third ball, Cinderella's fairy godmother appeared as soon the stepsisters had left.

When her fairy godmother touched her with the magic wand, Cinderella found herself in the most splendid and magnificent gown. It was made of silver and gold lace. On her feet were sparkling glass slippers.

Cinderella was so delighted that she hardly knew how to thank her fairy godmother.

"Enjoy yourself, my dear," said her fairy godmother, "but do not forget the time."

When Cinderella arrived at the ball in her dress of silver and gold, she looked so magnificent that everyone was speechless with astonishment.

The prince danced with no one but Cinderella all evening. Cinderella was so happy that she forgot all about the time.

Suddenly, the clock began to strike twelve. Cinderella rushed out of the door in such haste that she lost one of her slippers.

The prince ran after her and saw the slipper. He picked it up. It was small and dainty and made entirely of glass.

By the time Cinderella reached the place where her carriage had been, it had disappeared and she was in her old clothes. This time she had to run all the way home.

The prince looked everywhere for her, but could not find her. He still did not know her name, but he had fallen in love with her and he was determined to marry her.

So, the next morning, the prince took the glass slipper to the king, and said, "No one shall be my wife but she whose foot will fit this glass slipper."

The king's herald was sent through the streets of the city, carrying the small glass slipper on a blue cushion. The prince himself followed, hoping to find the lady with whom he had danced.

Every lady who had been to the feast was eager to try on the slipper. Each one hoped that the slipper would fit her and that she would marry the prince. Many ladies tried to squeeze their feet into the slipper, but their feet were too large for such a dainty shoe.

At last, the herald, followed by the prince, came to Cinderella's house.

Each of the stepsisters was determined to squeeze her foot into the tiny slipper, so that she could marry the prince. But they both had large, ugly feet. Even though they struggled, neither one could force her foot into the slipper.

At last, the prince turned to Cinderella's father and asked, "Have you no other daughter?"

"I have one more," replied the father. Then the stepsisters cried out, "She is much too dirty. She cannot show herself."

But the prince insisted and so Cinderella was sent for.

Cinderella seated herself on her stool, drew her foot out of her heavy wooden shoe, and put it into the slipper, which fitted like a glove.

When Cinderella stood up and the prince looked at her face, he cried out, "This is my true bride."

At that moment, Cinderella's fairy godmother appeared and turned her once more into the beautiful princess. The old grey dress became a velvet gown.

The prince lifted Cinderella on to his horse and rode away with her.

The stepsisters were horrified to discover that Cinderella was the beautiful princess who had been at the three balls. They were so angry that they were pale with rage.

At the palace, the king arranged a magnificent wedding for the prince and Cinderella. All the kings and queens and princes and princesses in the land came to the wedding. The wedding feast lasted a whole week.

And so Cinderella and the prince lived happily ever after.

Puss in Boots

Retold by Vera Southgate M.A., B.COM
with illustrations by Daniel Howarth

ONCE UPON A TIME there was a miller who had three sons. He was so poor that when he died he left nothing but his mill, his donkey and his cat.

The mill, of course, had to be left to his eldest son. The donkey went to his second son. Then all that was left for the youngest son was his father's cat.

"Alas!" sighed the youngest son, "Puss is no use to me and I am too poor even to feed him."

"Do not worry, dear master," said the cat. "Give me a pair of boots and a bag and you will find that we are not as badly off as you think."

The miller's son was very surprised to hear a cat talk. "A cat that can talk is perhaps clever enough to do as he promises," he thought to himself.

So, with his last few coins, the miller's son bought Puss a pair of boots and a bag.

Puss was delighted with the boots. He pulled them on and strutted up and down in front of his master. He looked so proud of himself that the miller's son could not help but laugh at him.

From that time onwards, the miller's son always called him Puss in Boots.

Then Puss slung the bag over his shoulder and went off to the garden. There he gathered some fresh lettuce leaves, which he put in his bag.

Next, Puss in Boots set off across the fields. He stopped when he came to a rabbit hole. Then, leaving the mouth of his bag open, he lay quietly down nearby.

A plump rabbit soon peeped out of the hole. It smelled the fresh lettuce leaves and came nearer. They were too tempting. First the rabbit's nose went into the bag and then its head. Puss quickly pulled the strings and the rabbit was caught.

With the rabbit in his bag, Puss in Boots marched off to the palace and asked to see the king.

When he was brought before him, he made a low bow and said, "Your Majesty, please accept this rabbit as a gift from my lord, the Marquis of Carrabas."

The king was amused by this cat wearing boots and talking. "Tell your master," he said, "that I accept his gift and I am much obliged."

On another day, Puss again lay down, as if he were dead, in a field. Once more his bag was open beside him. This time he caught two fine partridges.

Again, Puss in Boots took his catch to the king. As before, the king accepted the gift from the Marquis of Carrabas. He was so pleased with the partridges that he ordered the cat to be taken to the royal kitchens and fed.

As it happened, the king had a daughter who was said to be the most beautiful princess in the world.

One day, Puss in Boots heard that the king and his daughter were going for a drive along by the river. Puss ran immediately to the miller's son and said, "My master, if you will now do as I tell you, your future will be made."

"What would you have me do?" asked the miller's son.

"Come with me, my master," replied Puss, and led him to the bank of the river.

"There are only two things I want you to do," said the cat. "First, you must bathe here in the river. Secondly, you must believe that you are not yourself but the Marquis of Carrabas."

"I have never heard of the Marquis of Carrabas," said the miller's son, "but I will do as you say."

While the miller's son was bathing in the river, the royal carriages came into sight. The king was in his carriage with his daughter beside him. His nobles were riding behind.

Suddenly they were startled by a cry of "Help! Help! My lord the Marquis of Carrabas is drowning!"

The king, looking out of his carriage, could see no one but Puss in Boots, who was running up and down beside the river. However, the king told his nobles to run quickly to help the drowning man.

Puss ran back to the king as soon as the nobles had dragged his master from the river. Making a low bow, he said, "Your Majesty, what shall my poor master do, for a thief has stolen his clothes?"

Now, the truth was that Puss in Boots had hidden the clothes under a large stone.

"That is most unfortunate," said the king. "We cannot leave him there without clothes." So he gave orders to a servant to fetch a suit from the palace.

When the miller's son was dressed in a suit of good clothes, he looked a very fine man indeed.

The king then invited him to go for a drive with them. So the miller's son sat in the carriage beside the princess.

Puss ran on quickly, ahead of the carriage. He stopped when he reached a meadow where the mowers were cutting the grass.

Puss spoke to the mowers. "The king is coming this way and he may ask you whose meadow this is. Unless you say that it belongs to the Marquis of Carrabas, you shall all be chopped as fine as mincemeat."

The mowers were simple fellows and they were terrified to hear a cat talking in such a fierce voice.

161

A few minutes later, the king and his nobles drove by. As the king passed the large, lovely meadow, he stopped his carriage and spoke to the mowers.

"Tell me," he asked, "who owns this fine meadow?"

"It belongs to the Marquis of Carrabas, your Majesty," replied the mowers.

At that, the king turned to the miller's son. "You do indeed own a fine meadow, my lord," he said.

Meanwhile, Puss had run further on along the road. He reached a cornfield in which reapers were busy cutting the corn.

"The king will soon drive by," said Puss to the reapers. "He might ask whose cornfields these are. Unless you say that they belong to the Marquis of Carrabas, you shall all be chopped as fine as mincemeat."

The reapers, just like the mowers, were terrified to hear a cat talking in such a fierce voice.

165

A few minutes later, the king and all his nobles came into sight. Once more the king stopped his carriage.

"Tell me," he said to the reapers, "who owns these cornfields?"

"They belong to the Marquis of Carrabas," replied the reapers.

"What a rich man he must be and how handsome he looks," said the king to himself. "I do believe he would make a good husband for my daughter."

Now the fields really belonged to an ogre and this ogre lived in a castle a little further along.

Puss in Boots hurried along the road until he reached the castle. Then he knocked on the door, which was opened by the ogre himself.

"Sir," said Puss, "I am on a journey and, as I have often heard how wonderful you are, I have taken the liberty of calling to see you."

The ogre was startled to hear a cat talking. Yet he was pleased to learn that the cat had heard how wonderful he was. He immediately invited Puss into the castle.

"I have heard," said Puss, "that you can change yourself into any animal you choose."

"That is true," replied the ogre, and he instantly changed himself into a lion. Puss got a terrible fright. He quickly scrambled to the top of a very high dresser, out of harm's way.

At once the ogre changed himself from a lion back to an ogre again, whereupon Puss jumped down.

"Sir, I must tell you that you frightened me," said Puss. "Yet it must not be too difficult for such a big fellow as yourself to change into a large animal like a lion."

"It would be even more wonderful if a huge ogre could change himself into a tiny animal," went on Puss. "I suppose you could not, for instance, change yourself into a mouse?"

"Could not!" cried the ogre. "I can change myself into anything I choose. You shall see!" Immediately, he became a little grey mouse, which scampered across the floor in front of Puss in Boots.

With one spring, Puss pounced upon the mouse and gobbled it up. So there was an end to the ogre.

By this time the king's carriages were arriving at the castle. Puss in Boots, hearing the carriage wheels, ran to the gate. Bowing low, he said, "Welcome, your Majesty, to the castle of the Marquis of Carrabas."

"What, my lord!" cried the king, turning to the miller's son. "Does this castle also belong to you? I have nothing so grand in my whole kingdom."

The miller's son did not speak but gave his hand to the princess to help her from the carriage.

They all entered the castle where they found a wonderful feast ready to be served. It had been prepared for guests whom the ogre had expected. Fortunately, the ogre's friends did not arrive, as news had reached them that the king was in the castle.

The king and the princess, the nobles and the miller's son all sat down to the feast. Puss in Boots stood by the side of his master.

Every moment the king became more and more charmed with the miller's son. When the feast was over, the king said to him, "There is no one in the world I would rather have as my son-in-law. I now make you a prince."

Then the prince said that there was no one in the world he would like so much for his wife as the princess.

And the princess said there was no one in the world she would like so much for a husband as the prince.

So the two were married and lived happily ever after, in the ogre's castle.

Puss in Boots was very happy, living in the castle. He was always the greatest favourite with the king, the prince and the princess.

Never again had Puss to hunt for a meal. He lived on the fat of the land until the end of his days.

Snow White
and the
Seven Dwarfs

Retold by Vera Southgate M.A., B.COM
with illustrations by Gavin Scott

ONCE UPON A TIME on a cold winter's day, as the snowflakes were falling softly and swiftly, a queen sat sewing by her window.

As she sewed, the queen pricked her finger and three drops of blood fell upon her sewing.

The red of the blood against the white of the snow, framed by the black wood of the window frame, looked so beautiful that she thought, "Oh, how I wish I could have a child with skin as white as snow, with cheeks as red as blood and with hair as black as ebony!"

183

Now it happened that some time afterwards, the queen did have a baby daughter whose skin was as white as snow, whose cheeks were bright red and whose hair was as black as ebony. The queen called her little girl Snow White.

Unfortunately, soon after her child was born, the queen died. A year later the king married again.

The new queen was very beautiful but much too proud of her own beauty.

Often she stood in front of her magic mirror and asked, "Mirror, mirror, on the wall, who is the fairest of them all?"

185

The mirror, for it could only speak the truth, always replied:

"Thou, my Queen, art the fairest of them all!"

Meanwhile, Snow White was growing into a beautiful young girl. One day it happened that, when the queen stood in front of her mirror, it said:

"The truth I must speak and I vow, that the child Snow White is more lovely than thou."

When the queen heard these words, she was angry and jealous. Hatred for Snow White filled the queen's heart. She commanded a huntsman to take Snow White into the forest and kill her.

The huntsman led Snow White deep into the forest. When he stopped and drew out his knife to kill her, the poor child wept and begged him to spare her life. "Please do not kill me," she pleaded.

When the huntsman saw the tears on such a young and beautiful face, he took pity on her. He put away his knife and let her go free.

Snow White ran off into the great forest. She did not know which way to go, nor yet what would happen to her. She heard the roars of wild animals and she ran on and on. By evening, her feet were sore, her clothes were torn and her arms and legs were scratched.

Just as Snow White was ready to fall down with weariness, she came to a little cottage. She knocked on the door. There was no reply. She tried the door and it opened, so she went inside to rest.

Everything inside the cottage was small and neat. Against the wall stood seven little beds, each covered with a white bedspread.

Snow White was tired and longing to sleep. She tried six little beds but none suited her until she came to the seventh, which felt just right. She lay down and soon she was fast asleep.

Now the cottage belonged to seven dwarfs who had spent all day in the mountains, digging for gold. As they entered their cottage that evening, they noticed that their beds were not as neat as when they had left them.

"Look who's in my bed!" the seventh dwarf called to the others. The dwarfs stood around the bed together and gazed at the beautiful girl, sleeping soundly. As the dwarfs were anxious not to waken Snow White, they tiptoed away and ate their suppers very quietly.

In the morning, when Snow White first awoke and saw the seven dwarfs, she was rather frightened. The dwarfs, however, spoke kindly to her and when she told them her sad tale they were full of pity for her.

"If you will look after us," they said, "you can live here and we shall take care of you."

However, the dwarfs gave Snow White a warning. "We are out all day, working. If your stepmother learns that you are here, she may try to do you harm. So be sure to let no one into the house."

Snow White promised to be careful.

Meanwhile the queen believed Snow White to be dead. So it was some time before she asked her magic mirror:

"Mirror, mirror, on the wall, who is the fairest of them all?"

She could not believe her ears when she heard this reply:

"Snow White is living still,
and though thou, my Queen,
art certainly fair, this child's great
beauty doth make her more fair."

Great was the queen's anger when she heard these words. She determined to find Snow White and kill her herself.

The queen disguised herself as an old pedlar-woman. Then she travelled to the dwarfs' cottage, knocked on the door and shouted, "Laces and ribbons for sale!"

"What harm can this poor old woman do to me?" thought Snow White. She opened the door and chose some pretty pink laces for her corset. The old woman offered to lace up Snow White's corset for her. Snow White, suspecting nothing, agreed.

The queen laced Snow White so tightly that she could not breathe, and she fell to the floor as if she were dead.

The dwarfs were shocked to find their beloved Snow White lying on the floor. When they saw how tightly she was laced, they cut the new laces. Soon she began to breathe again and gradually the colour returned to her cheeks.

The dwarfs were convinced that the old pedlar-woman must have been Snow White's wicked stepmother. They again warned Snow White to take great care.

The queen hurried back through the forest filled with joy. When she reached the palace she went straight to her magic mirror.

When the queen asked the usual question, the mirror replied:

"Snow White is living still,
and though thou, my Queen,
art certainly fair, this child's great
beauty doth make her more fair."

The queen was enraged. She prepared a poisoned comb, disguised herself and travelled to the dwarfs' cottage. She knocked on the door and shouted, "Pretty things to sell!"

Snow White put her head out of the window. "I have promised to open the door to no one."

"Never mind! You can look," replied the queen, holding up the dainty comb.

Snow White could not resist it and she opened the door.

"You must let me comb your hair properly for you," the old woman said. The queen then stuck the comb sharply into Snow White's head so that the poison went into her blood. She fell to the floor, as if dead.

When the seven dwarfs found Snow White lying on the floor, they suspected that her stepmother had been again. They soon found the poisoned comb and pulled it out.

Once more they begged Snow White never to open the door while they were out.

Later the jubilant queen asked her mirror:
"Mirror, mirror, on the wall,
who is the fairest of them all?"

Just as before, the mirror replied:

*"Snow White is living still,
and though thou, my Queen,
art certainly fair, this child's great
beauty doth make her more fair."*

At these words the queen stamped her
feet and beat on the mirror in her rage.
"Snow White shall die," she vowed, "even
if it costs me my life!"

The queen knew that it might prove impossible to persuade Snow White to let her into the cottage a third time, so she plotted cunningly.

She took a lovely apple which had one green cheek and one rosy cheek. Then she put poison into the red cheek of the apple, leaving the green side free of poison. This time, she filled her basket with apples and disguised herself as a farmer's wife.

For the third time, she made her way to the dwarfs' cottage and knocked on the door.

"I am forbidden to open the door to anyone," said Snow White.

"I only want to get rid of these apples," replied the farmer's wife.

"I dare not take one," replied Snow White, shaking her head.

"Are you afraid that it's poisoned?" joked the farmer's wife. "Look, I'll cut it in two and we shall each eat half."

She held out the poisoned rosy half of the apple to Snow White and bit into the green half herself.

When Snow White saw the woman happily eating one half of the apple, she took the rosy half of the apple and bit into it. No sooner had she done so than she fell down dead.

The queen laughed a horrible laugh. When she returned to her palace, at long last her mirror said:

"Thou, my Queen, art the fairest of them all!"

The jealous queen was finally content.

When the dwarfs returned home in the evening, there lay Snow White on the floor, no longer breathing. They unlaced her corset, combed her hair and washed her face, and yet they could not revive her.

The dwarfs were heartbroken. They knew they must bury their beloved Snow White but they could not bear to do so.

The dwarfs had a glass coffin made, in order that they might still see Snow White. Then they each took it in turn to sit by the coffin, day and night.

There Snow White lay, as if still alive, but sleeping, with her skin as white as snow, her cheeks as red as blood and her hair as black as ebony. Even the birds came and wept to see her lying so still.

One day, it happened that a prince found the glass coffin. He fell in love with the beautiful girl inside.

"Let me have the coffin," he begged the dwarfs, "and I will give you whatever you ask."

But they only answered, "We would not part with Snow White for all the gold in the world."

"If you will give her to me," pleaded the prince, "I shall cherish her all my life."

At length, the dwarfs took pity on the prince and agreed to give him the coffin.

As the prince's servants were carrying the coffin down the mountainside, they stumbled on the roots of a tree. The coffin was so badly jolted that the piece of apple, which had stuck in Snow White's throat, was flung out. She opened her eyes, lifted up the lid of the coffin and sat up.

The prince was overjoyed to see her alive. "Come with me to my father's palace and we shall be married," he begged. Snow White agreed, for she had fallen in love with him instantly.

She said goodbye to the dwarfs who had loved her so dearly. Although they were sad to lose her, they knew that she would be happy.

It happened that Snow White's stepmother was among those invited to Snow White's wedding. Dressed in her finery, she stood before her mirror and asked:

"Mirror, mirror, on the wall, who is the fairest of them all?"

The mirror replied:

"The truth I must speak and I vow, that the young bride-to-be is more lovely than thou!"

The angry queen felt that she must see this beauty. When she arrived at the feast and saw Snow White, her rage was so great that she fell down and died instantly.

And Snow White and the prince lived in peace and happiness.